Notes for Parents

Learning to read is a tremendous challenge for each child. Children need to succeed, not only for their own deep satisfaction, but also to gain approval. Success in children's early learning experiences mostly depends on adults who have time and who care.

Never underestimate the value of reading stories and rhymes to children. It is only through pleasurable experiences that they grow to understand what books have to offer.

Time for reading

Try to establish a regular routine so that your child has your undivided attention for a few minutes each day while you share books together.

★ Read each book *to* your child and talk about the story and pictures.
★ Read each book *with* your child pointing to the words.
★ Listen patiently to your child *reading to you*. Give the words they stumble over.

Gold Star Readers – Level 1

Those children who are able to recognise some words in books and in their environment are ready to move to an early reading series such as Gold Star Readers, which offer:

★ stories full of fun and action so that they can be read many times;
★ rhyming text to help early reading;
★ stories which are neither too long nor have too many words on a page;
★ pictures to help children guess what the words say.

Enjoy this reading time together.
—Betty Root,
Reading Consultant

D0230157

A Reader's Digest® Children's Book
This edition first published 2000 by Reader's Digest Children's
Publishing Ltd, King's Court, Parsonage Lane, Bath BA1 1ER,
a subsidiary of The Reader's Digest Association, Inc.
Copyright © 1999 Reader's Digest Children's Publishing, Inc.

British Library Cataloguing-in-Publication Data.
A catalogue record for this book is available from
the British Library.

ISBN 1-84088-273-5

Who Loves Me Best?

by Kirsten Hall
illustrated by Chris Demarest

Gold Star Readers

Reader's Digest Children's Books

I love my friend.

He loves me, too.

He's my best friend.

Can you guess who?

He's not too big.

He's not too small.

He does not talk
or sing at all.

He loves to jump.

He loves to run.

He loves to play.

He's always fun.

He loves the park.

He loves to chase.

He always beats me when we race.

He always greets me
at my door.

He's always hungry.

More! More! More!

He'll be my dog
when I grow up.

So, did you guess?

My friend's a pup!

Colour in the star next to each word you can read.

☆ a	☆ greets	☆ pup
☆ all	☆ grow	☆ race
☆ always	☆ guess	☆ run
☆ at	☆ he	☆ sing
☆ be	☆ he'll	☆ small
☆ beats	☆ he's	☆ so
☆ best	☆ hungry	☆ talk
☆ big	☆ I	☆ the
☆ can	☆ jump	☆ to
☆ chase	☆ love	☆ too
☆ did	☆ me	☆ up
☆ does	☆ more	☆ we
☆ dog	☆ my	☆ when
☆ door	☆ not	☆ who
☆ friend	☆ or	☆ you
☆ friend's	☆ park	
☆ fun	☆ play	